Mrs. Goose's Baby

To the Underwoods

Published by
Dell Publishing
a division of
Bantam Doubleday Dell Publishing Group, Inc.
666 Fifth Avenue
New York, New York 10103

This work was first published in 1989 in Great Britain by Walker Books Ltd.

The trademark Yearling® is registered in the
U.S. Patent and Trademark Office.
The trademark Dell® is registered in the
U.S. Patent and Trademark Office.
ISBN: 0-440-40615-3
Reprinted by arrangement with Little, Brown and Company Inc.
Printed in the United States of America
April 1992

10 9 8 7 6 5 4 3 2 1
LBM

Mrs. Goose's Baby

Charlotte Voake

A PICTURE YEARLING

One day Mrs. Goose found an egg

and made a nest to put it in.

She sat on the egg

to keep it safe and warm.

Soon the egg started to crack open.

The little bird inside was
pecking at the shell.

Mrs. Goose's baby was very small.
She was fluffy and yellow.

Mrs Goose took her baby out
to eat some grass.

But her baby didn't want to eat grass.
She ran off to look for
 something different.

Mrs. Goose took her baby to the pond
to teach her how to swim.

But her baby just sat on the shore.

 Mrs. Goose's baby grew

and grew

and grew.

Mrs. Goose's feathers
were smooth and white.

Her baby's feathers were brown.
They weren't smooth at all.

Mrs. Goose had large webbed feet.
Her baby had little
pointy toes.

The baby followed Mrs Goose everywhere,
and cuddled up to her at night.

Mrs. Goose loved her baby very much
and kept her safe from strangers.

Mrs. Goose's baby never did
eat much grass.

HONK!

The baby never did go swimming
in the pond.

And everyone except Mrs Goose knew why.

Mrs Goose's baby was a

CHICKEN!